Leaving Tra...

The Gold...

By: K.M.

THE GOLDEN YEARS

First edition. November 18, 2024.

Copyright © 2024 K.Moore.

ISBN: 979-8227175878

Written by K.Moore.

Also by K.Moore

.

Bonded By Love
Bonded By Love (Malcolm)
Bonded By Love (Harmony's Story)

Leaving Trauma Behind
Leaving Trauma Behind

Leaving Trauma Behind: Family Growing Pains
Family Growing Pains

Leaving Trauma Behind: The Golden Years
The Golden Years

Leaving Trauma Behind: Turning a new Leaf
Turning a new Leaf

Table of Contents

Book 4 | Volume 1 1

Dedication 3

1 | Prepping for wedding #1 4

2 | Giving Thanks over family Dinner 7

3 | Four months until wedding #1 13

4 | Three months until the wedding..................................... 16

5 | Injured by the enemy 19

6 | Two months til Wedding #1 22

7 | The States star witness.. 25

8 | Last minute wedding prep and court date set................ 29

9 | Traveling to the Caribbean 32

10 | 2 Honeymoons.. 37

11 | Trial day is here... 41

12 | The continuation and verdict in the case..................... 44

13 | Return from honeymoon... 48

14 | One month later 51

15 | Dress shop dilemma 54

16 | Eight months til the wedding....................................... 57

17 | Five months until the wedding 60

18 | 90 days and counting 63

19 | 3 arrive and 1 leaves 66

20 | Wedding Day... 72

21 | A reception and a proposal... 76

22 | Another execution and 2 honeymoons......................... 80

23 | The Final chapter 85

This book is for those who have overcome trauma to become better than before. Never stop chasing your dreams. As long as you beleive then you can acheive.

Book 4
Volume 1

For more information, or to book an event, contact :
relatablefictionwriting@gmail.com
http//www.[1]relatablefictionwriting.com
Book design by Nakeia Davis
Cover design by Canva
ISBN - Paperback: 9798227175878

First Edition: June 2024

---

1.   http://www.website.com

Dedication

To all my fiction Lovers
    Once you find your spiritual guide, let them lead you on your path to righteousness. Let your Love shine bright through the darkness of the night. Stand hand and hand in the face of despair while showing those around you how much you care.

K.Moore

1

Prepping for wedding #1

Now we get to enjoy a life of peace and quiet with our 5 couples from this series. Every Friday night they get together for group dates that are filled with fun. Newly added to the mix we have 3 more couples who spend Saturday nights following in the footsteps of the veterans of the dating game. Leading up to their weddings Cora and Max along with Regina and Rashad tried to spend as much time around Zeek and Kahlani for marriage advice.

Ramona and Chef Jean as well as Janette and Michael are more of what we all strive to become in our senior years. One lovely Black woman and Hawaiian Black woman who overcame trauma at the hands of bad men, to find their way to happiness. Two Handsome Black men with the compassion, strength, knowledge and patience to love their women right.For the modern day couples Zeek and Kahlani are the image of what we strive to acheive. And our future couples are being led by the image of Malcolm and Kapri.

Now with a wedding coming up in 7 months all the couples in this series are going to give us all more highs and some lows of overcoming trauma to ending on a triumphant side of life. Moving forward to finishing off the planning with Janette and Ramona, we take a detour the weekend of Nov 25, 2021. All the kids are out of school and wanting to spend time with their grandmas. Harmony walked into her parents home asking her grandmas"What's left to do before the wedding Grams"?

Well baby girl your grandma Janette has been debating with me for weeks on what food we should have, Ramona said shaking her head. GRANDMA are you trying to cheat on Pop Pop with the caterer, Harmony exclaimed? Just then Malcolm and Kapri walked into the kitchen asking" What's going on everybody"? Our grandma's are having a disagreement about the catering for their wedding, Harmony explained.With a smirk Malcolm asked"Is Janette making the caterer uncomfortable with her flirting like she did for mom and dad's wedding"?

With a laugh Ramona replied"No" we just can't decide what type of food to have at the reception. Janette wants to have southern comfort food and I want to add some Hawaiian style foods from my family, Ramona said starting to tear up. Malcolm and Harmony both went over to embrace Ramona offering their opinions on the matter. Harmony looked at Malcolm then at Ramona saying " aren't you marrying a Chef " TuTu Wahine? Followed by Malcolm saying" have him make some of your traditional favorites this weekend for the holiday so grandma can try them".

That's a great idea let me go call him now to see if he's up for it? Sitting by the front door Ramona dialed Chef Jean and he answered after just one ring. "Aloha nani" Hello beautiful what can I do for you, he asked? "Aloha u'i" Hello handsome I have a question for you about Sunday dinner, Ramona replied. Then she asked; would you be willing to make some island traditional meals for the family to try before the wedding? Without hesitation Chef Jean replied; I'd be happy too nani,let me go make the menu. The two sat flirting for another 5 minutes before hanging up.

2
Giving Thanks over family Dinner

Ramona excitedly went back into the kitchen to inform everyone of the good news. Meanwhile, Chef Jean was at the local market with Zeek explaining what he was going to make for them. Man are going to really make some of the food Lani's grandparents made for us during our trip, Zeek asked excitedly? Son, I sure am going to do just that, you know like I know when your lady asks for something that's within your grasp, your immediate response is a no brainer. If it makes my lady happy to eat my cooking, I'll cook and feed her everyday if I have to, Jean said with a smile.

I certainly do understand what you mean, I think I've shown Lani that I put her happiness and safety before my own. Then I try to show my sons and my friends how to keep a woman happy, Zeek stated with pride. Now let's head to the house to feed the family. Back at the house most of the food was done and put aside. Chef Jean now had free reign over the kitchen at the Williams home. Within 2 hours Chef Jean had the entire neighborhood smelling like a Hawaiian Island.

Two days later on Nov 27, 2021 it was time to sample some cultural deliciousness. Kahlani, helped by Harmony, set the table for the family and guests. Once everyone was seated and grace was said Janette started with her questions about the food on the table. Poor Michael nearly choked on his water.

Janette: I know what most of this food is but, I'm curious as to what this is in the foil and collards over here

Chef Jean: with a slight chuckle replied, it's "Lua Lua" a Hawaiian staple Janette. It's pork butt, butter fish and sea salt steamed in foil or Tea Leaves.

Janette: Ok but what is this pink bloody looking meat on top of the rice?

Ramona: That is "Poke" . It's Salmon marinated in soy sauce, sesame oil, seaweed, avocado and edamame. It's served over rice with mac & cheese on the side. It is raw but still good and it's a delicacy of the big island in Hawaii.

Janette: Now somebody tell me why we have eggs with brown gravy on rice?

Kahlani: Ma, this is "Loco Moco " it's a hamburger dipped in tabasco on a bed of rice. Then it's covered in brown gravy and topped off with a fried egg. Traditionally it's served for breakfast but we're going to have it for dinner.

Janette: Fine but why are there uncooked doughnuts and what are these blocks of white grits doing on the dessert table?

Harmony: Trying to control her laughter said to Janette; Grandma I helped TuTu Kane make them. The doughnuts are called "Malasadas" and they are baked, not fried and filled with fruit jam. And those are not grits, they are "Haupia" Coconut Pudding Bars.

Once everyone had eaten and was about to clean off the table Janette stopped Chef Jean and joyfully stated: You're in charge of the food for the wedding, this dinner tonight was delicious. Janette I've got some other ideas for the wedding but you'll have to wait and see everything, Jean replied. All the ladies went into the kitchen to help Kahlani clean up before parting ways for the night.

For the next month Janette and Ramona were on the phone everyday with Kahlani. Finishing the planning of this wedding was just a comedy show with Janette. Now Ramoona understood why Kahlani almost canceled her wedding after dealing with Janette's planning. Every week it was something new that she didn't like about it. Then Janette loved to brag about her best friend marrying a Chef and she herself was marrying a (retired) cop. Everyday Ramona and Kahlani have to remind her that no one cares what those men do or did for a living.

After being reprimanded Janette would apologize and take down her posts on social media. Now we all know that at 60 this woman has no business on social media acting like she's still in her 20's. Michael walked over to Janette sitting on the couch of their new home asking: What's on your mind sweetheart? Can I ask you a question Mike, Janette said with a somber look on her face. Sure baby you can ask me anything he said reaching out to hold her hand. Then Janette asked: Am I too extra with my actions all the time?

Baby you are just being yourself and that's what attracted me to you. You're just going to have to be more mindful of how you act around certain people, Mike replied. And baby don't post other people's business on social media, let them rave about their own victories on social media. Hearing this from her own fiancee was hard to accept, it was easier hearing this type of criticism from Zeek was hard enough.

By the time Dec 25, 2021 Janette and Mike sent gifts for all the kids. Zeek and Kahlani have been telling her since their wedding that they don't celebrate birthdays or holidays. But they were able to open the gifts the next day and called Janette to thank her. A week later everyone around the world was celebrating the New Year while Zeek was turning 38 in 2022. With 5 months until his mother's wedding Zeek thought maybe he should give Mike and his soon to be father in law a bachelor party.

Janette wasn't happy about that unless they could have a joint bachelor and bachelorette party. Kahlani made a suggestion that they just have a date night with the two couples. Now Janette was happy and the men were in agreement so date night it is. On Friday Jan 5,2022 the three couples met at SpaceAge Bowling Alley with Harmony & Travion and Jazzlene & Dametrius in tow. Everyone enjoyed their battle of the sexes game. It was amazing for Zeek and Kahlani to see their mother's finally having fun with men who loved them wholeheartedly.

That is until Janette started thinking that the young girl at the concession stand was trying to talk her way into Mike's bed. Both Zeek and Mike went over to understand the situation and stop Janette from making the poor girl quit her job. Ma, why are you over here yelling at this young lady, Zeek asked with concern. This so called young lady is over here making goo goo eyes at my man and doing too much blushing in his direction, Janette stated hysterically.

Ma'am I meant you no harm at all, I was just being polite to everyone in your party, the young girl explained. After that the couples went to World Tavern for dinner and boy did Janette get checked by everyone at the table about her behavior. Why must you make a big deal out of the smallest things Janette, Ramona asked? So, you think I'm just being extra all the time Janette asked looking at everyone at the table. In unison everyone replied "YES" leaving Janette stunned.

Zeek spoke up again saying: You're always making yourself the center of attention when it's not necessary, you almost made Lani cancel our wedding because of your actions. Now you're making my mother in law uncomfortable about sharing a wedding with you. While we're all here just tell us what's the reason for you acting so brash all the time? Janette began by saying: Son, after the way your dad treated me I just feel like I don't deserve him and that he'll leave me if I calm down.

Stunned to silence, all the ladies were emotional after hearing her statement . Mike turned to Janette cupping her face in his hand saying: baby I've had my time to play with young girls when I was young. I have no need for a younger woman. I'm right where God wanted me to be with the woman just for me.The rest of the men at the table followed his lead turning to their ladies asking in unison "Do you believe me"? With a nod of "YES" from the ladies each man planted a kiss on his woman's lips.

Once dinner was over each couple went their separate ways for the night. With 5 months until the wedding and Feb 14th fastly approaching, all the couples wanted to hang out more often. Especially now that Malcolm had some free time in his schedule and Kapri finally had a day off from the hospital being a nurse on the graveyard shift. Even Rashad & Max had some time off to spend with Regina and Cora. One night all the couples went out for Karaoke and had a great time watching Ramona and Janette perform their hearts out.

Before the night was over all the ladies turned to Kahlani and asked: Will you sing with us to close out the night? Then all the employees glanced at her saying: We love hearing you sing on date night with your husband, how about one more. So Kahlani stood to her feet grabbing the hands of her mother and mother in law heading straight for the stage again. And all together the ladies sang a classic by Sister Sledge "We are Family".

Each of the men sat watching their ladies beam with radiance as they sang their hearts out. The ladies had every person in the building on their feet until the end of the song. It's amazing to see 8 Black Men supporting their Black Women having a great night out. On the way out of the bar, a blast from Zeek's past walked in saying: Bro how you been I haven't seen you since High School. That voice belonged to none other than Ja'kiel Knight Zeek's right hand man.

After a brotherly hug Ja'kiel asked Zeek what he'd been up to since they left school. You know man I just been working, got three more kids and this is my wife Kahlani, Zeek stated gleefully. I see y'all out here celebrating, is it your anniversary Ja'kiel asked? No man, we're having a joint bachelor/bachelorette party for my mom and mother in law with their fiancee's, Zeek explained. Congrats Ja'kiel said to the happy couples before turning to Zeek saying: I see you heading out so we'll catch up some time when you're free.

Yeah man we sure will do that, I gotta get this lady home before she starts to worry about the kids. Alright you guys have a goodnight, Ja'kiel replied. Have a goodnight Zeek and Kahlani responded on the way out the door.

3

Four months until wedding #1

After reuniting with a loyal friend Zeek had a great time catching up every week. March 5, 2022 the men went to a bar for a drink and some small talk. While at the bar a woman was staring at the two of them with a seductive smirk. Ja'kiel noticed that Zeek continued to give this woman some major "side eye" at the bar. Jakiel asks: why do you keep looking over there, do you know her or something? Zeek's face grew stern as he replied; Yeah she went to high school with my wife. Had Lani drugged and raped the night of senior prom and left her for dead in a hotel. Now she used her adopted son to try and drug my daughter 6 months ago at senior prom.

Appalled by what he was hearing Ja'kiel stood to his feet to walk over but was stopped by Zeek. Let's just wait and see what she has/wants to say Ja, Zeek replied. As the two men looked at each other Danella approached them with a drink in hand taking a seat next to Zeek. I noticed you watching me from the other end of the bar and decided to come over to introduce myself to one and reintroduce myself to the other, Danella said with seduction in her voice. Zeek looked at her with disgust in his eyes saying: There is nothing you have to say to me after what you've done to my wife and daughter.

With a smirk Danella placed her glass on the bar and replied: I was so close to ridding the world of those two beauties so men would acknowledge me more. But that wife of yours just won't go away so I figured I'd go after someone close to her in the form of your daughter. At this point both men were offended so Ja'kiel turned to Zeek asking: What's your next move man? The real question is what's her next move ,Zeek replied looking Danella in the eye? Don't worry I'll get rid of both of them and anyone else who gets in the way of me having a hot cop for a husband, Danella replied leaning in to kiss Zeek just as Ja'kiel stepped in front of him to receive the kiss.

Noticing she had kissed the wrong person Damella gagged with disgust and ran out the bar. The two men then shared a laugh and parted ways for the night. As he arrived home Zeek found Lani getting ready for bed fresh out of the shower. Once in the bed Zeek decided to let his wife know about his run in with Danella. A mixture of disgust turned to laughter as Zeek told the story of Danella kissing Ja'kiel and thinking it was him. Before turning over Zeek explained: Baby remember when we got together and at our wedding(s) I promised to protect you at all costs. Yes handsome I remember is there something I need to be worried about?

Well baby I have to work extra shifts for a while to ensure our families safety. Danella is going to continue trying to harm you and Harmony, maybe even Camille. She told me and Ja that she is only doing this out of jealousy for how men faun after you and not her. She also wants to marry me after she kills all the women in my life. At this point Lani was irritated and just wanted to get rid of all these petty women in her life.

4

Three months until the wedding

By March 30,2022 Kahlani and Janette were on the phone with Ramona having some girltalk. Do you believe we have 90 days until our wedding, Janette asked the ladies? I was just thinking about that this morning and I can't wait, Ramona stated excitedly. Kahlani replied somberly: I'm so excited for both of you. Ramona, knowing her daughter well, asked: what's wrong with you baby, you sound like you're crying. Well mom I am worried about something and maybe I'm just overreacting but I'm scared.

What's got you so worried, daughter in law, Janette asked with concern? Well Zeek and I recently found out that an old rival of mine from High School has gotten out of Prison. And she's planning to kill me and the kids to have Zeek all to herself. She's already had her son attempt to drug and kill Harmony. Are you serious I'm going to tell Mike so all the guys can get you and the kids extra security, Janette stated before hanging up.

Oh God I'm so sorry baby I'll call her and tell her to leave it alone, then I'll call you back, Ramona said. Mom don't bother, she's right we do need extra security,Kahlani replied. Zeek,Malcolm,Rashad and Max could use his expertise to ensure our safety. Alright daughter I'll leave it alone, Ramona said somberly before hanging up. With worry on her mind Kahlani went to make dinner when the front window was busted from the outside.

On instinct Kahlani dialed Zeek as she made her way toward the living room. Y'all know Lani wasn't going into danger empty handed. Reaching into the drawer next to the kitchen door Lani grabbed Mrs.Johnson's gun that she never told Zeek she had or got rid of. While creeping into the living room Zeek's voice came on the line saying " Hey beautiful I'm on my way home to you. Hysterically Lani shouted "someone is in the house, the front window is broken". I have to get up stairs to the twins, she said bursting into tears.

Baby stay calm I'm almost there but if you have to fight put up the best fight possible. When the line went dead Lani put her game face on and put her phone away. Just as she turned the corner into the living room the sound of snarky laughter came from the intruder. To Lani's surprise the voice belonged to none other than Danella.

5
Injured by the enemy

"Danella " why are you in my house with a gun, Lani asked, incensed by Danella's audacity. So your husband didn't tell you the plan, Danella laughed while pointing the gun at Lani.

Danella must be slow because she didn't even notice Lani was pointing a gun at her the whole time. Why don't you tell me the plan since you're here Danella, Kahlani stated uninterested. So you didn't know I've been on a mission to kill you since you had me put in prison. Danella, that was 19 years ago you're 37 holding a grudge against me after the crime you committed against me, that's so stupid, Kahlani said.

You don't get it do you Kah-La-ni, you get the life everyone else wants and think no one will be envious. That's just petty and you know it Danella, we were kids back then Kahlani exclaimed. It doesn't matter when it was, what matters is that you got everything I wanted. And after today I'll finally get what I want in the form of you dying and me spending the rest of my life with Officer Williams. Zeek overheard the whole conversation as he entered his home with cuffs and service weapon ready. Just as he entered the living room "boom boom" two shots rang out.

Both of the ladies had shot each other with Kahlani being hit in the left shoulder and Danella was hit in the chest. Zeek radioed for Rashad to get an ambulance at his house. What's going on at your house Zeek, Rashad asked concerned? That crazy girl Danella has broken into my house and shot Lani. the kids are OK, just get me some help here. Now Shad. Baby stay calm I'm going to get you some help don't die on me. By the time the ambulance arrived Danella was begging for Zeek to save her and Kahlani was unconscious on the way to the hospital.

An hour later both ladies were in stable condition with the bullets removed. Once Danella woke up she was hysterically asking for Zeek to come to her room. The nurse gave Zeek the message after checking Kahlani's vitals before leaving to make her rounds. Zeek leaned down to whisper in Lani's ear " I'll be back in a minute baby". Danella wants to speak to me about something but I'll be back, then he was gone. In room 421 Danella sat in her bed smiling after the nurse gave her the message that Zeek was on his way to see her. Two minutes later Zeek knocked on the door frame to get Danella's attention.

Seeing Zeek at the door made Danella fill with glee as she looked up. Zeekey, thank you for coming to see me handsome, Danella said sweetly. First of all you are not my mother, so don't ever in your life call me Zeekey. After hearing him speak in such a menacing tone toward her Danella had to think fast before he could leave, So Zeek now that I've gotten rid of Kahlani we can be together. I'll even help raise those little demons of yours and we'll enjoy our golden years as husband and wife.

In disbelief Zeek replied: My wife isn't dead and I'm headed back to her room with my "little demons" to get her ready to go home. And you'll be heading to a different home once you're discharged from here Danella. Noticing she'd said too much, Danella tried to retract everything she'd just said which offended Zeek. But it was too late for Danella to save herself from what happened next. Mike walked in with the new Chief of Police Curtis Alexander along with Max and Rashad. Chief Alexander spoke first saying: Danella Watkins you are under arrest for (2) counts of attempted murder of Kahlani and Harmony Williams. (4) counts of premeditated murder of Christian,Camille,Brandon and Ann Marie Williams.

How do you know it was me that did all these things you speak of, Danella asked suspiciously? Zeek pulled out his phone and pressed play for all to hear her speaking her plans for the future. Michael spoke up saying: This recording is the nail in the coffin for you. You will never be good enough for my son in law. Then Zeek looked over at Danella as he walked out the door saying: You're paying a hefty price for petty jealousy.

6

Two months til Wedding #1

By April 26, 2022 Kahlani was in physical therapy for her shoulder injury. She was still in shock that another person from her past was trying to kill her again. Lord please let us get through the wedding before going through another court case, Kahlani recited these words in her head throughout her therapy session. She was determined to get better so she could dance with her husband at both this year and next year's weddings.

Back at the house all of the kids were worried and asked Zeek the same question"What are we going to do about our safety"? Zeek looked each of his children in the eye and replied: I'm your father and I always make a wrong situation right. Then he turned to Malcolm and placed a strong hand on his shoulder saying: Now that you're on the force it's your job to help me, Pop Pop and your uncles ensure the safety of this family. With a head nod Malcolm understood the assignment before him. Before Zeek could walk away Malcolm stopped him to say: Are you heading to the jail because I have some questions for Ms. Watkins. With a look of assurance in his eye Zeek nodded saying "Let's Go Officer Williams".

At the Jail Zeek andMalcolm were surprised to see Michael was already there waiting. After greeting him with a hug Malcolm asked: Pop Pop why are you here shouldn't you be making sure grandma doesn't want to change anything else for the wedding? With a chuckle Mike replied: Janette isn't going to change anything except the food and that's for Jean to deal with. But I'm here because Chief Alexander called saying that Danella wanted to speak to us motioning between himself and Zeek. That's cool I'll wait in the hall but I do have some questions of my own for Ms.Watkins before we leave here today.

In the interrogation room Danella sat cuffed to the chair waiting for Zeek and Michael. 10 minutes later the door opened and they walked along with Malcolm in uniform. Zeek spoke first asking: What do you want to speak with us about Danella? **Danella:** Well Zeek I wanted you to know personally that I won't be in prison for long after we go to court.

Malcolm: Do you know how dumb you look right now? You do know that everything spoken in this room is recorded and you just gave us all the information we need to intercept your plan?

Michael: Who else is in on this plan with you to escape and commit this murder spree?

Danella: Oh just a couple people that hate Kahlani with a passion. Once we get rid of her, your kids and mom(looking at Zeek) and her mother, the plan will be complete.

With a menacing glare Zeek looked Danella in the eye asking: Who is "WE" that you speak of?

Danella: Oh I'm sure you know Melody Stanton and Destiny Richardson.And I'm sure Kahlani has mentioned my friends from high school Calvin Donaldson and Alexis Mitchell. Well Jessica Stuart decided to bail on us once she got released on parole.

Malcolm: You either tell the whole plan or tell where Jessica is now. Either way you're never getting out to finish your plan.

Danella: Well your put of luck officer because I've said too much as it is. But as for Jessica she was living across the street from me at 7009 Melrose Dr. I don't know if she skipped town yet.

———— ⟨⟩ ————

With that information the men left the room heading toward the exit. Once outside Malcolm asked Michael if he would drop him off at the station to pick up his patrol car. Of course I will but why do you need your patrol car are you on night shift? Yeah Pop Pop and I wanted to stop by that address to speak with Jessica Stuart. Michael looked at Malcolm with admiration saying: that's some good police work you're doing son "I'm proud of you". The men hugged and went their separate ways. After clocking in and getting into his patrol car Malcolm drove over to 7009 Melrose Dr to speak to Jessica Stuart.

7

The States star witness

Malcolm got no answer on his first visit to Jessica Stuart. But a week later on a wim Malcolm tried again and got the chance to talk with her. Upon opening the door Jessica was instantly worried about why a cop was at her home. Nervously, Jessica asked Malcolm "What can I do for you today Officer"? Ms.Stuart I'm Officer Williams may I come in and ask you a few questions? Jessica nodded, stepping aside motioning for him to come in.Upon entering Jessica offered Malcolm a glass of water to which he politely declined.

Sitting at the dining table Malcolm asked Jessica 1) What is the motive behind Danella's actions? 2) What made you decide not to be a part of the plan? 3) Can you tell me what the whole plan was? 4) When was it supposed to take place? 5) Do you feel in danger by speaking with me today? With her head hung low, holding her teacup Jessica began to speak. 1) Her motive is mostly jealousy and insecurity when it comes to Kahlani. 2) I decided that after what we did to Kahlani in high school and being in jail let me know that I didn't want to go back. 3) The plan was to get rid of everyone that makes her feel unattractive. And anyone who is in the way of her having the man of her dreams. 4) If she goes to jail now the plan will be executed the day after her conviction. 5) To be honest with you I've never felt safe with Danella and Calvin loose on the streets. Not to mention the fact that they're in contact with Alexis Mitchell who is locked up with Destiny Richardson and Melody Stanton right now.

Shocked by the information he just received, Malcolm thanked Jessica for talking with him before making his exit. Malcolm called Michael and Zeek on three way at the station. What's going on both men asked in unison worried what Malcolm had to say. Then he told them everything Jessica told him about the plan. So, we need to also ensure Jesica's security before the case goes to trial. She feels that Calvin and Danella are going to do something to her for talking to the police. Zeek chimed in to say: I'll call Rashad and Max to set up a security detail for her. Thanks for the information son me and your dad will track down Calvin to stop this plan from taking place, Michael replied.

May 3, 2022 the security detail was sitting in front of Jessica's home when a suspicious car pulled up. One of the officers called Max to get a black and white to come pick up this suspicious person. Just as the officer hung up the phone the person walked up to the front door with what looked like a weapon. Looking around cautiously the male figure heard the sound of a camera flash to his right. As he turned around a patrol car showed up to make the arrest and it just happened to be Officer Malcolm Williams. The person he was picking up happened to be Calvin Donaldson. What a surprise.

Once at the jail Malcolm took the lead in asking questions of Calvin. 1) Why were at the home of Jessica Stuart today? 2) Were you planning to kill her so she couldn't testify in court? 3) Was this your idea or Danella's to target Jessica? 4) What is your purpose for targeting my stepmom Kahlani Williams? And don't play games with me or lie to me right now, Malcolm said with a menacing glare.

Stunned, Calvin sat back looking Malcolm in the eye with a smirk. Then he began to talk saying: Your father married that pass around after I had my way with her in high school. At this point Malcolm was starting to get annoyed. Now Calvin, seeing he was not very entertaining to Malcolm he decided to answer the officer's questions. 1)I was at Jessica's house today to send a message from Danella. 2) Yes I was going to kill her, that was the message from Danella for talking to the cops. 3) as you may have guessed it was Danella's idea the whole plan was. 4) My purpose in targeting Kahlani was to get her out the way for Danella and for the money.

"What money" Malcolm exclaimed in a stun regarding Calvin's admission. Danella promised us we would split a total of $15000 after the murders were done. By we I mean myself, Danella, Alexis, Destiny and Melody. Curiously Malcolm asked how would Alexis, Destiny and Melody benefit or even use their portion of the money. If Danella hadn't gotten caught she was going to put their money on their books for them. I don't know where she got the money or where she's hiding it but that was the plan.

With that Malcolm went to call his dad and inform him of what was going on with the case. So you're saying that since Alexis is locked up with you and Harmony's mothers they stand to gain something in the end, Zeek asked. Yeah dad that's what both Jessica and Calvin have told me. Alright son we'll get extra security for the family as we prepare for your grandma's wedding. Hopefully the courts will have the trial after the wedding and not have a speedy trial in the next 30 days.

8

Last minute wedding prep and court date set

On May 20, 2022 a call came in from the county jail to Zeek and Malcolm was at his dad's home to intercept the call. On the other line was a member of the DA's office with a message for the family. The message was clear as day saying: Destiny and Melody will be getting Life in prison for being an accessory to commit murder. Alexis will be getting an additional 25 yrs added to her infractions from her current sentence that would have ended in 5 yrs. Calvin will be getting 50 yrs for the attempted murder of Jessica Stuart and the members of the Williams family. As the mastermind of the whole thing Danella will be getting the death penalty.

This news was just what Malcolm wanted to hear for his family. Then the person on the other line said: the date of the trial will be scheduled for July 11, 2022. After thanking the young lady Malcolm called his dad with the news. Now we can relax knowing they won't have a chance to harm our family. Don't get too excited son they could be trying to come up with a new plan as we speak. But I am glad they made the court date after the wedding. That's true dad and since it's my day off I'll head over to Kapri's house to hang out, I'll talk to you and mom later, Malcolm said happily. Talk to you later son, Zeek replied before hanging up.

On the other side of town Zeek and Kahlani were with Janette/Michael and Ramona/Jean making sure their suits and dresses were ready to take on the plane for the wedding. To their surprise Michael and Jean's suits needed some extra tailoring before they could leave the state. After leaving the tailorZeek told Michael what Malcolm had informed him about the case. Michael was bummed that he wouldn't be in town to see the trial for himself. Don't worry I'll send you the information on the low while mom is distracted, Zeek said with a smirk.

Y'all know the only thing that will distract Janette is being on the phone with Ramona. Let's hope that Ramona will be interested in talking to her friend while she's on her honeymoon with Jean. But we'll find out for ourselves when we get to that chapter. But we need to see if

Janette can get any more entertaining than she has been in the last two books. Let's get back to the action in the conclusion in this series.

Two days later the tailor called saying that Michael and Jean's suits were ready. Zeek volunteered to go pick them up for the two grooms on his way home from the station. On his way out Max stopped Zeek saying: man one day we need to have a men's day and talk. Rashad and I have no idea what we're getting ourselves into when it comes to marriage, Max said with uncertainty. Alright, man when we finish with the most comedic wedding of the century, I'll set y'all up with our therapist for some couples therapy.

Once Zeek made it home with the suits in hand and gave them to Jean and Michael he let them know what Max said to him. When you two come back from your honeymoons we need to help the other two grooms get ready for their wedding next year. I figured that we'd have a few weeks of couples therapy with them and the girls. Jean and Michael glanced at one another then shrugged saying: I'm good with that idea. Maybe we'll need a therapist to help us deal with Janette's antics before, during and after the wedding, Michael said with a chuckle.

Man, you got that right but I still don't know how you put up with my mom and her antics, Zeek said laughing. Son I don't know either, maybe I'm just a man in Love, Michael said with a smile. I agree with you 100% Mike, I feel the same way about Ramona and I know Zeek feels the same way about Lani, Jean replied. Yeah, man that woman is truly my better half on any given day, Zeek responded.

9

Traveling to the Caribbean

Now it was time to make their way to the Caribbean for the union of Janette Marie Jackson & Michael Joseph Byrd and Ramona Kapule Ka'uhane & Jean Kai Kekoa. Now knowing that finally all the people out to do them harm were off the streets Zeek and Kahlani could pack and get to the airport. Once on the plane Zeek was shocked to see Rashad & Regina along with Max & Cora seated. What are you guys doing in this fight, Zeek asked? We're coming to the wedding Janette and Ramona invited us, Cora exclaimed. Just as the plane was about to take off Kahlani spotted Malcolm & Kapri, Harmony & Travion along with Jazzline & Dametrius sitting behind her. I guess the whole Williams Clan is coming to this wedding. This will be the best couples retreat ever, Kahlani shouted just as the attendant asked her to have a seat.

With 2 weeks until the wedding the couples had daily excursions around the island. They did a lot of couples activities including some couples therapy. During one of the activities Janette was asked by the tour guide "What attracted her to her fiance"? Janette being her over the top self started being extra. Janette started trying to undress Mike while saying " this man right here is just like me" isn't he fiiiiine ladies? In a fit of laughter all the girls were rolling on the sand while the men were feeling awkward by the scene.

Two days later the event planner called asking for Chef Jean to come speak to the caterer about the food list. Just as he finished at the reception site Jean headed back to the resort to rest. Just as Jean was getting to his room the sound of Janette yelling could be heard down the hall. What's going on Ramona asked, sticking her head out of the door? I'll go check on her, Jean replied with Ramona in tow. As they got to the end of the hall, Janette was firing one of their servers from the catering company.

The whole resort could hear Janette yelling " You mutated cockroach looking heifer" you thought you were going to sneak into my room to have sex with my man. I know and trust my man, he would never want a trash bag like you when he has a real woman right here. In a fit of embarrassment the whole family walked back to their rooms chuckling at Janette's words. Every room on their floor was filled with the laughter of strangers as well as the wedding party for the entire night.

By the time June 30,2022 arrived everyone was on pins and needles except Janette. Not one person in the resort knew what to expect from Janette after the scene in the hallway 3 days earlier. After Kahlani made sure the site on the beach was ready for the ceremony to begin. Regina and Cora went over to the reception site in the resort making sure everything was just right for the two happy couples. At 2pm it was finally time for these two lovely couples to be wed on the beach.

Both Michael and Jean stood under the archway awaiting the arrival of their brides. The processional of the wedding party began with Zeek and Kahlani the maid of honor & bestman. Followed by the flower girl Camille and ring bearer Christian. Bringing up the tail end were the other couples in their group as the wedding party. Lastly, the two beautiful brides stepped out onto the beach to meet their grooms. On the left was 61 yrs young Janette in her off-white halter column dress. And Ramona on the right in her Ivory strapless trumpet gown.

The ceremony lasted 30 minutes with both couples reciting their own heartfelt vows to each other. The minister asked for the rings as the Hawaiian interpreter spoke in Niihau for Ramona and Jean. Camille walked up with both hands out in front of her presenting the rings to both of the ministers. As she turned to take her seat Camille looked at her grandparents saying :Aloha wau iā ʻoe (I Love You). Everyone on the beach was in tears at hearing this beautiful little girl speaking her mother's native tongue. Then it was time to kiss the beautiful brides and both Mike and Jean didn't hesitate to show their love for their brides.

While the resort crew was cleaning up the beach everyone headed inside to the reception site for the party. In the banquet hall were crystal chandeliers with every table and chair covered in satin with baby blue ribbons & baby blue table runners. Once all the guests were seated and the bridal party entered, it was time for the two brides and grooms to enter. As they took their seats the DJ asked for the best man and maid of honor to give their speeches. Being the gentleman he was meant to be, Zeek told his wife to go first.

Kahlani: To both of my moms and dads I'm not going to refer to you as in-laws at all. Janette you've been the most hilarious person I've ever known other than Cora and Regina. You even shared a great man in the form of a son that I get to spend the rest of my life with. Now Mike I'm sure my husband has already told you but, I'm going to tell you again " We don't know how you manage to put up with Ma". I personally will pray for you and your sanity throughout your marriage. Now Jean I'm truly grateful for you coming into this family. My mom, like myself, has been alone a long time not feeling worthy of love. But you and Mike are the representation of a dad I wish I had as a little girl. And lastly, makuahine(mother) it's been me and you against the world my entire life. Now I can rest easy knowing we both are in good hands. You've already been resting easy since I got married. To all of you Aloha wau iā ʻoe (I Love You).

Zeek: Mom and Pop this is not only a great day for you but for me as well. Now my mother can stop being so nosey in the love lives of me and my kids. Even though we will miss mom's hilarious dating stories. Pop you and I have a father/son bond that transcends all the way down to the bond I have with Malcolm in our profession. It warms my heart to know that myself, Rashad and Max aren't the only people my kids can go to for legal advice. Now to my in-laws : everytime I look at you two I see myself and Kahlani. Jean, here's a piece of advice for you sir, I want you to take this information to heart. When I met Lani I used to cook all the meals. Once I married her she started telling me to get out of her kitchen. So be ready for Mona to tell you the same thing when y'all get home.

After sharing in the laughter of both speeches it was time for dinner to be served. Just as requested, Chef Jean made sure everyone had a menu to feed their souls. For the appetizers: Baked Taco Cups and Chipotle Chicken Wings & Side Salad. For the Entree and 2 Sides: Beef and Broccoli stir fry, Pineapple Chicken w/Kale Slaw and asparagus, Ribs w/ glazed carrots and fresh corn. Jean even made sure there was pizza for the kids. For dessert: Guava Chiffon Cake for the adults and 7-layer Jello for the kids.

Before the party could get started Kahlani grabbed Harmony, Kapri and Jazzline for the bouquet toss. Being in on the surprise Harmony and Jazzline didn't put any effort into catching either bouquet. Everyone watched as Kapri caught the bouquet from Janette and Camille caught the bouquet from Ramona. Just as Kapri turned to show Malcolm the bouquet, he was down on one knee with a 4-carat heart shaped ring in hand. With eyes full of emotion and all eyes on her Kapri without hesitation shouted Yes 3x. This is how you start a party so together the newlyweds and the newly engaged couple led everyone into a night of dancing and congratulations.

10

2 Honeymoons

The next day everyone was packing up for check-out by 11am to catch their flights. By the time everyone made it to the airport heading for separate terminals, they all hugged and asked Malcolm & Kapri to inform them when they chose a wedding date. Once on their plane Zeek closed his eyes finally feeling at peace then he remembered the court trial was in 10 days. Noticing her husband's unease, Kahlani placed a comforting hand on his arm saying: we've endured much worse babe. We can't go anywhere but up from here after this hopefully final time in court.

With that Zeek laid his head back on the seat and closed his eyes for a much needed rest. When he opened his eyes Camille was pulling on his wrist saying: come on daddy I want to get home. By the time the Williams Family made it home Zeek sat on the porch and thanked Jehovah for giving him the strength to endure all his trials and being triumphant against his enemies. Even the fact that the house next door was still a part of his family. A piece of Mrs.Wilson left to him which he shared with his 3rd baby mama as well as his mother and now his oldest child is living there with his fiance'.

Just as Zeek was about to go into the house his cell rang with a call from his mom. Surprised to be receiving a call from Janette, Zeek asked her how was newlywed life? Knowing his mother Zeek sat back down to prepare for the story Janette was about to give him.

Janette: After the situation with that "Mutated Cockroach" the Virgin Islands tried to sleep with Mike the day before our wedding. You'd think people would stop trying to set me off but,Noooo even the heifers in Mexico are trying me Son.

Zeek: Taking a breath he asked: What could they possibly have done to set you off ma?

Janette: So when we landed we had our bags taken up to our room so we could go get some food with the locals. When we got back to the resort an hour ago the housekeeper was in our room. But she wasn't cleaning that miniature big mac was in the room, unpacking "My Husband's" clothes and sniffing his drawers.

Zeek: Unable to control himself Zeek laughed so loud the whole neighborhood came outside to see what happened. Ma I know you're just exaggerating there is no way that lady did any of that stuff in your room.

Janette: Oh it's true Son just listen to your Pop out on the balcony still laughing about the whole thing. Walking over to the balcony Janette handed Mike her phone saying: here tell our son what you are laughing at.

Michael: Still laughing he replied " Baby it's not that serious" then turned his attention to a laughing Zeek on the phone. Son everything she said is true, she just didn't tell you the part I'm laughing at. Maybe your mom should have joined the force because her interrogation methods are hilarious to watch first hand. Man your momma started whopping that poor girl in the room and all the way into the hall. Then she started chasing the girl with the cleaning cart down the hall. By the time they got to the end of the hall your momma had tripped the girl 4 times with the cart. The girl was so scared that she confessed to your momma where she hid everything she had stolen from guests at the resort.

Zeek: Pop I can't even breathe at this point I have no idea what we can do about mom. Enjoy the rest of your honeymoon and don't worry about the trial in 9 days. We'll talk about the details when you get back. Then they hung up.

During dinner Zeek told the story to the family and everyone was on the floor in fit of laughter over Janette being so extra. Ramona face-timed Kahlani in a fit of laughter regarding Janette.

Kahlani: Hey ma how is the move going?

Ramona: It's going great and thanks to your mother in law we got a chance to take a break and laugh. All the furniture in the house now and the movers will be bringing the POD to the house tomorrow so we can unpack our dishes and clothes.

Kahlani: That's good to hear I'm so happy for you mom. I'm glad to see you truly happy just like me. I'm sure you're tired, go rest and enjoy your man just as I'm going to do with your son in law.

Ramona: Okay daughter I Love You, Goodnight

Kahlani: Goodnight mom I Love You too

Four days later Zeek received a call from one of his colleagues on the force saying that Danella wanted to speak to him and Malcolm before the trial. Knowing this could be a bad idea Zeek decided to ask Malcolm for his thoughts on the idea. Since we'll be in there together I don't see anything wrong with the idea dad, Malcolm said walking out of the house. The father and son duo drove to the jail to meet with Danella. Noticing his father's unease, Malcolm asked Zeek what's on his mind. Zeek replied; It's just that I'm used to being the one in the driver's seat so to be driven around by my first born is a heartwarming moment in time for me.

Once at the jail and seated in the interrogation room both men waited for Danella to say why she wanted to speak to them. And with an evil smirk Danella told the two Williams men that she wouldn't rest until Kahlani was dead and gone. Even if the Judge sentenced her to death she'd survive long enough to witness the day her enemy went to her grave. Malcolm looked over at his dad saying: This crazy woman needs to be admitted to the same hospital "TuTu Wahine" was in all those years. Overhearing the conversation Danella answered saying: I don't need medical help I need that mixed mutt erased.

Now hearing this Zeek was instantly offended but he remembered what Mrs. Wilson told him as a child in **Deut 32:35** Vengeance is mine, and retribution, At the appointed time when their foot slips, For the day of their disaster is near, And what awaits them will come quickly. Then Zeek walked out of the room with his son in tow. In 5 days Danella's tirade will be over and the world will be safer.

This is the home stretch in our journey of Leaving Trauma Behind. Let's get this trial over and see the Williams Family inspire us to keep enduring to the end. These will be the longest 5 days of Zeek's life in his mission to protect his family. Everyone, let's continue to cheer for our hero Ezekiel Roger Williams to the end of time. That's enough of an intermission, it's time to get back to the story.

11

Trial day is here

Finally July 11, 2022 is here and the Williams family is the most excited. No more looking over their shoulders for fear that someone is out to do them harm. All of the kids wanted to go to the trial but were stopped by Zeek saying: only Malcolm and Harmony would be going. With Travion and Malcolm along with her dad at her side Harmony felt brave. But when they arrived at the courthouse and Harmony saw her uncles Max and Rashad she just knew victory was within her grasp. Upon entering the courtroom even Travion's dad Raymond was sitting in the gallery.

Once everyone was sworn in and the defendants were brought in it was time for opening statements. Then it was time for the state to call their first witness which happened to be Harmony.

Prosecutor: Ms.Williams how did you come to know of Ms.Watkins?

Harmony: I went on a date with her adopted son Dametrius

Prosecutor: During that date was the defendant present the entire time?

Harmony: Yes she was

Prosecutor: During the date did the defendant act as though she were going to do harm unto you?

Harmony: No

Prosecutor: Have you had any contact with the other defendant Calvin Donaldson, if so "When"?

Harmony: Yes; the day after my date with Dametrius, he drove us to the mall.

Prosecutor: Thank you Ms.Williams, your witness counsel

D.A: Ms.Williams when you met the defendants did they give you their real names?

Harmony: No I was told their names were Danielle and Darryl Little

D.A: When did you find out their true identity

Harmony: When my mom called her by her government name at our family home. And that's when we found out that she had changed Dametrius's name after adopting him.

D.A: Did Ms. Watkins admit to anything else?

Harmony: Yes; she admitted that she and Mr.Donaldson along with someone named Alexis were plotting to kill my mom Kahlani Williams. They were planning to split the money with Melody Stanton and Destiny Richardson after killing Kahlani and myself. She also paid some students from my college to break into my apartment to assault me and my roommate.

D.A: How do you know she hired them to assault you?

Harmony: Because two of the young men were on the football team with my boyfriend Travion Smith and they confessed to him when he caught them trying to pick the lock to my apartment. The other two men were on the basketball team with Dametrius, they all know me and my roommate are dating Travion and Dametrius.

D.A: No further questions Your Honor

After hearing the testimony of this young woman Judge Anthony told everyone " We're going to adjourn for lunch and return in 2 hrs". After the judge walked back to his chambers Harmony walked over to her family and Travion in the gallery. They were all so proud of her testimony today. After hugging everyone both Zeek and Travion told her, she could go home and come back for the afternoon session. Harmony happily agreed and asked Travion to take her home?

12

The continuation and verdict in the case

2 hours later the court reconvened with the state calling Jessica Stuart to the stand. The prosecution started with their questioning which seemed like an open and shut case for the state.

Prosecutor: Ms.Stuart what's your affiliation with the defendants?

Jessica: I went to highschool with the defendants and Kahlani Williams.

Prosecutor: What is your connection to Mrs.Williams?

Jessica: I participated in the kidnapping and rape of Kahlani along with the defendants?

Prosecutor: What was your role in that crime against Mrs.Williams?

Jessica: I along with Alexis Mitchell and Ms.Watkins held Kahlani down while Mr. Donaldson savagely raped her.

Prosecutor: What was your punishment for your part in the crime?

Jessica: I along with the other defendants was given a life sentence with the possibility of parole in 25 yrs with good behavior.

Prosecutor: No further questions; your witness counsel

D.A: Ms.Stuart you said you were given a life sentence; what were your charges against Mrs.Williams

Jessica: Attempted Murder, False Imprisonment, Stalking and the Murder of Kahlani's unborn child

D.A: After your conviction did you have any animosity toward Mrs. Williams up to this day?

Jessica: Not at all; I accepted the outcome for my actions

D.A: When you were released early what was your first interaction with the defendants?

Jessica: Danella was still angry about it and wanted Kahlani dead at any cost. Since she couldn't find her, the two defendants went to an orphanage to adopt a child. That's where Dametrius comes into the picture, they changed his name to little and changed names as well.

D.A: How do you know they changed that young man's name?

Jessica: She brought the paperwork to my house. I even took pictures of the paperwork for my own records.

D.A: Do you have those photos with you today? If so can you present them to the court?

Jessica: I do have them with me today, here you go counsel (handing the photos to the Judge) who hands them to the D.A after looking.

D.A: Did the defendants tell you anything else while at your home?

Jessica: They asked me if I would help them come up with a plan to kill Kahlani. To which I declined and Danella wasn't too happy about that.

D.A: What gave you the idea that she wasn't happy with your answer?

Jessica: Danella said since I didn't want to help I must be on friendly terms with Kahlani and want to die as well.

D.A: Did you have any inclination that Ms. Watkins was going to go through with killing you within the last month or so?

Jessica: No not until Officer Williams came to talk to me about the plot. Then I heard the S.W.A.T team arresting Mr. Donaldson outside my home. The next day Officer Williams came back to tell me that Danella wanted Calvin to kill me for not helping them kill Kahlani.

D.A: No further questions your honor

With that Judge Anthony allowed the jury to break for deliberation. From the stand Judge Anthony shook his head in disbelief of how jealousy, envy and greed have led people to such lows. It was so disappointing to see the number of targets on the backs of the Williams Family in his courtroom. Then he looked out into the gallery making eye contact with Zeek, taking a much needed breath said: Mr. Williams it pains my heart to keep seeing your family in my courtroom. Almost every case I've had in my career has surrounded your family. Hopefully today will be the last time we have to be in here for a trial. With a head nod Zeek agreed with Judge Anthony just as the jury reentered the courtroom.

This time without asking the jury foreman stated: Your Honor we have come to an agreement on the verdict. Then the paper was passed to the bailiff who passed it to Judge Anthony. Judge Anthony took a quick look at the verdict then looked at the defendants. He proceeded to say to them: the two of you along with your co-conspirators are the lowest form of human matter on earth. The crimes you've committed against this family can not be forgiven and for that I'm given the task of sentencing you at this time. So Danella Watkins and Calvin Donaldson for your crimes and violating the terms of your parole you are sentenced to **Death by lethal Injection**. Your co-conspirators who are currently incarcerated will also be getting moved to different prisons around the U.S until the day of their execution on death row. Court is adjourned.

13
Return from honeymoon

Back at the house everyone was breathing a sigh of relief that this family has peace of mind. Finally free of all Satan's dirty work that's been haunting them for nearly 4 decades. Two days later the phone rang with a call from Ramona asking Kahlani how the trial went. The trial was full of surprises but it went well, especially Harmony's testimony. Well hopefully they're done bothering you for good this time around baby, Ramona replied. They are all getting the death penalty for violating their parole, Kahlani explained.

Wow that's great news Ramona said with a chuckle. Mom, what's so funny? Kahlani asked, confused. Have you talked to your mother in law lately? She did call us when they checked into the resort but not for the last week. Why is there something we should know? I'm not going to say anything, maybe your father in law will be able to explain if he and Jean can stop laughing at Janette long enough to tell you. Oh Lord, I'll be ready for a good laugh when they get home in 3 days.

Three days later on the 14th of July Janette and Michael arrived at Zeek's home to a curious audience. Hello everybody Janette shouted walking into the living room. Then she asked, why are y'all looking at me like that? Both Malcolm and Harmony spoke up asking: Grandma what did "You" do in Mexico? Looking over at Michael who was already laughing she sighed and proceeded to explain. Well I'm sure my son told y'all what happened when we arrived.

So the next day we went to have our couples massage and the same miniature hamburglar looking heifer was in there too. The moment she thought I was gonna let her put her hands on my husband's body I sat straight up and went on attack. The problem was that I didn't have anything under the towel. So when I went after her the towel fell so I was beating her up butt naked in front of everybody at the resort in the lobby. This chick was so thirsty that on the 4th she tried to break into our room to go through my purse. But she didn't know I was in the bathroom so I snuck up on her just she was walking out the door with my purse.

I put her in a chokehold and let her scream until Michael came back with our food from the BBQ they were having on the beach. I did a full body search of her in the room before she could get away. And I found not one but three pairs of Mike's underwear tucked in this broads bra. And she had my license and 3 of my credit cards in her pocket. So I started beating her again and realized I was about to commit a murder and Mike wasn't even going to stop me. He was just sitting there laughing like this was the best comedy show he'd ever seen. Needless to say she got hurt pretty bad and lost her job for stealing from the guests. The rest of the honeymoon was pretty much peaceful until 3 days ago.

The lady at the front desk was leaving love notes on our room service tray. Talking about how she thinks Mike looks good for his age and she wants to see him alone after I go to bed. So I sent her a note saying: Let's go on a date then. I showed up in the penthouse suite and started slapping that girl all over every room in that suite. Where was Michael while this was happening, Kahlani asked between laughter? He was standing in the doorway laughing just like he is right now. Everyone was in tears from laughing except for Janette who didn't find anything funny about her honeymoon in Mexico.

There is nothing you can do at this point but shake your head at Janette. She means well but makes the smallest issues become the most hilarious form of conversation. Now that we have one wedding done it's time for us to get ready for our second double wedding. Let's finish the planning with Regina and Cora for the next 10 months. Maybe Janette will entertain us some more in this wedding as well.

14

One month later

On Aug 14, 2022 Kahlani was sitting with Cora and Regina making lesson plans for the upcoming school year. What classes are you teaching this year Kahlani, Cora asked. I'm teaching History and Art which I love. How about you two? Well I'm teaching Math and Science, Regina replied. Lastly, Cora replied I'm only teaching English this year. Why do you only have one course to teach this year Cora, Kahlani wanted to know.

Well I just found out that I'm due on March 10, 2023. Your pregnant Cora, Regina exclaimed with joy for her friend. In tears Kahlani happily hugged her friend along with Regina. This was an exciting moment for the friends. Not only were they having a wedding now they have a baby shower to plan for Cora. Do you know the gender yet? We can have a gender reveal during the baby shower, Regina shouted dancing around the table. First off I haven't told Max yet but we are having **"Triplets"**. No I don't know the gender yet so wait until next month when I find out then you can plan the shower.

After lunch the ladies parted ways to go to their respective homes. Upon entering her house Kahlani was met by her husband asking: What made you so happy today? Oh babe I just found out that Max and Cora are expecting Triplets 2 months before their wedding. But we can't say anything to Max about it until tomorrow because Cora hasn't told him yet. The following day at the station Zeek and Rashad congratulated Max on becoming a dad.

Man I'm excited and in a month we'll find out the gender, Max stated. I'll be glad so Regina can stop asking me what I think you're having, Rashad said laughing. I'm like woman I didn't make kids with him stop asking me that question. The men shared a laugh before getting back to the other topic of discussion. How are you feeling about all your enemies being executed in a couple years, Zeek, Max asked. I'm relieved, especially seeing Lani and Harmony feeling safer now. Do y'all know where those fools have been transferred to? Since Anthony said they wouldn't be able to correspond with each other after we left court, Zeek asked.

Yeah man he had each of them moved to different states and put in solitary so they can't socialize with anyone not even the guards. Destiny is in Florida while Melody is in Colorado and Alexis is in upstate New York. Danella is in Texas and Calvin is in Mississippi which surprised Zeek. I wonder why Judge Anthony chose those states for them, Zeek pondered. Well guess we'll be getting a call when each of them gets their last meal on earth.

15

Dress shop dilemma

By September it was time for Cora and Regina to pick out their dresses. It was the end of the first trimester for Cora and she wanted a dress she could slim down into in two months after having triplets. The first dress Cora tried on was an Ivory Satin Princess gown which made her glow. Then out of nowhere Janette said before you go to the check out try on this dress I picked up for you. In her hand was a beaded lace ballgown which all the girls cringe in disgust. But Cora tried it on just to keep Janette quiet. When Cora came out in the dress the first thing she said was " I can't breathe" get me out of this thing now. Out of nowhere Janette started laughing saying: I'm sorry girl I didn't mean to make you look like a pregnant elephant.

Kahlani shouted "Ma that's so insensitive of you" that woman is 3 months pregnant with triplets. In surprise Janette went back into the dressing room to hug and apologize to Cora. Baby I had no idea you were pregnant but know this it's a beautiful dress just not the one for you. Lastly Cora tried on an A-Line silk organza gown which seemed a better fit for Regina than her. Girl hang that dress back up so I can try it on, Regina replied before anyone could give their opinion of it on Cora. Which Cora did before trying on a Red cocktail dress and white belt for the reception which everyone fell in love with.

Now it was Regina's turn to try on dresses and she started with the silk organza A-Line. Instantly she was in love just like Cora was with the first gown she tried on. But she had to try on a couple others before making her decision. Second she tried on a Blush Empire waist dress which everyone agreed was OK but not for her. Lastly Regina came out in a strapless trumpet gown with an embroidered Red belt. This dress would be perfect for the reception but Regina wanted a cocktail dress for the reception as well. The sales woman brought out a white cocktail dress in the same lace material with the Red embroidered belt and it was a hit.

Next it was time to dress Ann Marie in her flower girl dress and the little princess didn't disappoint. Kahlani put her 9 month old in a Pick lace gown and that little girl's smile melted the hearts of everyone in the room. Then Kahlani remembered that in 9 months her daughter will need a bigger dress at 18 months. Do you know if this dress comes in an 18 months old size Kahlani asked the attendant? Let me go check for you, the attendant said and walked toward the stock room. When she returned with the dress in hand Kahlani shouted we'll take it.

Then it was Harmony and Jazzline's turn to try on their bridesmaid dresses. Their Column dresses had a Red corset bodice and white bottom with Red organza. The young ladies looked like grecian goddesses at the shop. After all the tailoring was done everyone parted ways for the evening. Back at the house Ann Marie ran to Zeek with open arms full of smiles. Heyy baby girl you have fun today with mommy and sister, Zeek cooed. Full of smiles both of his daughters and his wife gave him kisses in the living room.

By the time September rolled around it was time for the men to go to get their suits. Zeek takes Brandon to meet up with Dametrius, Travion, Max and Rashad. At the tailor each of the men tried on their suits in record time. Brandon was so handsome in his Grey suit with a Red bow tie. Max in his Red suit with a White cumberbun. Rashad in his White suit with Red cumberbun. Zeek looked like a king in his Burgundy suit with a matching Black bow tie & cumberbun. Lastly Dametrius and Travion looked like stars in their Black suits with (Dametrius's) matching Red bow tie and cumberbun (Travion's) matching White bow tie and cumberbun.

16

Eight months til the wedding

October was the start of Cora's 2nd trimester and time to meet the caterer for the wedding. This time Ramona went with them for the meeting. Janette tried her best to convince the girls to let her come with but, after what happened at the dress shop it was a "No". Cora didn't need any stress from Janette and her antics. Low and behold Janette managed to find her way to the meeting.

Seeing Cora with the start of her baby bump Janette walked over giving her a hug and promised to be on her best behavior. Once everyone was seated at the table the samples were placed before them. The caterer served each lady a plate before stepping to the side. The meal was quiet until Janette out of nowhere turned to Ramona saying "This food is bland, your husband makes better food than this". Then she turned to Cora and Regina saying " Just write down the stuff you like and give it to Ramona so Jean can give y'all good quality food.

Cora shook her head looking over at Regina then Lani saying "Y'all decide for me, I lost my appetite" then left. See what you did Ma this is why we didn't invite you Lani said frustrated. Janette looked around confused as to what she did wrong "All I did was state the fact that the food was bland and I wouldn't eat it unless Jean made it". Then Lani and Regina went over to Cora's house to check on her and make sure she had something to eat.

When she opened the door Cora looked worn out but to her surprise her friends brought the food from the tasting. The ladies sat down to sample the food alone together for an hour. Before Lani could leave Regina called Rashad asking that he and Max come to Cora's to sample the food. Once at home Kahlani told her family about the way Janette acted at the tasting. Meanwhile across town Max and Rashad sat with their ladies trying the food and agreed the food did need some seasoning. Then Max stated that all they needed to do was tell the caterer what seasoning to add to the food, not pester Chef Jean. Rashad agreed after Chef Jean made all the food for his own wedding due to Janette's theatrics over the food.

By 9:00 both couples parted ways for the night so Cora could get rest before her doctor's appointment. The next day Max took Cora to find out the sex of their triplets. In the office Dr.Thompson put the gel on Cota's abdomen and the first strong heartbeat filled the room and the couple looked at one another with smiles. Then the second heartbeat filled the room followed by the third. Maxexcitedly asked "Doc can you tell what we're having yet"? Of course I can sir just give me a few minutes and we'll have that information and some photos for you, Dr. Thompson replied.

After the doctor left the room the happy couple sat holding hands waiting for the news. Five minutes later Dr.Thompson came back holding a folder in his hand. Taking a seat in front of the couple Dr.Thompson said with a smile in 7 months you'll be meeting your son and 2 daughters. I have a son and 2 daughters ,Max said in shock. Boy am I glad to be a cop now I understand what Zeek is gonna endure with Camille and Ann Marie. Now Max was nervous and couldn't wait to talk with Zeek for some advice.

For the next month up to Thanksgiving Max was under Zeek watching how he interacted with his daughters. Zeek made it look so easy but he'd always tell Max " This is the fun/easy part of parenting in general". Then he'd say: wait until they get in school, that's when you'll need to keep the (gun,maze and pepper spray) close by. That made Max even more concerned about being a father. The part of raising a son was cool for Max, he'll have an extra set of eyes on his daughters as they grow up. Maybe even help him protect the girls, especially protecting Cora.

17

Five months until the wedding

Reaching the end of the fall season and everyone was getting ready to wrap presents for all the kids. Also Max and Cora were getting the nursery ready for their three little ones. And now that all the preparations for the wedding are done Regina and Kahlani can focus on the baby shower for their friend. On Dec 10,2022 the ladies had a beautiful "Royal" themed party planned for Cora and Max. All the men came dressed as the royal guards for the day. All the ladies came dressed as ladies in waiting while Cora was Queen for the day.

Every game was filled with a medieval times theme from the men participating in archery to find out the gender of the babies. The ladies played backgammon to guess if Cota would have her son or one of the girls first. Even the kids got in on the fun playing "skittles"(bowling) in the corner. Once everyone ate and opened the gifts the men helped Max take the gifts home. The ladies stayed behind to help clean up the event space then they took Cora home before retiring to their own homes.

By the time Dec 25th came around our favorite family was gathered together in Zeek's home having dinner and laughing at all their moments with Janette over the years. Kinda makes you wonder what Janette will act like at the wedding but we'll all have to wait and see for ourselves. With 5 months until the wedding and only 96 days til Cora is due. What else could our group of friends endure leading up to our 2nd double wedding. On Jan 1, 2023 in the mail was a letter addressed to Mr& Mrs Williams from the Florida Women's Prison.

Reading the letter together Zeek and Kahlani noticed that the letter asked if they wanted to attend Destiny's execution on April 10, 2023. Her date was moved up due to her trying to correspond with her other defendants in other states. The two of them looked at each other and agreed if Harmony wanted to go. So Kahlani Facetimed Harmony to see what she wanted to do. Harmony said of course she'd want to go and would put it on her calendar. At least they know they'll be able to make it to their friend's wedding without any interruptions.

Nine days later another letter came, this time it was from the Colorado State Women's Prison. Now they were asking if they would be attending the execution of Melody. They moved her date up to June 14,2023 due to her trying to bribe an officer to help her escape again. Why must people allow the devil to lead them down the wrong path in life and end up like these people in this story? Even in solitary confinement these delusional people are still trying to ruin Zeek and Kahlani's lives. Could this be Roger's way of torturing them from the grave?

Not only does this couple have to fly to Florida with their eldest daughter for her mother's execution. But now they will be accompanying their eldest son Malcolm to Colorado for his mother's execution. Let's hope the other three can hold off until later this year to screw up. Just as February started all of our couples got together to enjoy each other's company and plan out what to do for their group dates for the month. By the 16th another letter came to Zeek and Kahlani from the Texas Women's Prison saying that Danella was found dead in her cell. Apparently she couldn't live in isolation knowing she couldn't torture Kahlani from the inside or even escape to accomplish her mission to commit murder. The next day a knock at the door got Kahlani's attention as she was putting the twins down for a nap. On the other side of the door Jessica stood nervous of how Kahlani would react to her showing up at her home.

Once she opened the door Zeek and Malcolm had walked out from the kitchen to get the door. In shock Kahlani asked Jessica why she was there at the Williams home? Jessica nervously stated "I wanted to know if you received a letter from the prison about Danella"? Yes we did receive a letter yesterday but, I don't understand " what could have made her snap like that". Can I come in so I can explain it to you?

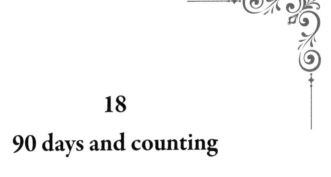

18
90 days and counting

Kahlani stepped to the side to welcome Jessica into her home to explain. Once seated Malcolm offered Jessica a bottle of water. After accepting it Jessica proceeded to explain "I called the prison after reading my letter to get an understanding". The prison Psychologist explained that after their session Danella didn't agree with anything the doctor told her. The doctor told Danella she couldn't contact you or me (Letters, Calls, etc) and she couldn't have any contact with Dametrius. Then the doctor lastly told that the truth of Dametrius's biological mother would be revealed to him. That was the last straw for Danella and she went back to her cell and hung herself with a bed sheet.

Everyone nodded their heads in understanding of everything Jessica just told them. Then she turned to Kahlani saying: I know who Dametrius's biological mother is. Well who is it? That young man is so lost not knowing his true identity or where he came from, Zeek replied anxiously. Jessica closed her tearfilled eyes and replied: I am his mother and Calvin is his father. Stunned, Kahlani asked: did Danella know Calvin was the father? We both knew Danella was very possessive over Calvin so we told it was some other guy from high school, Jessica replied. Since she was getting released before me, I asked her to find out what foster home he was in and take care of him until I was released. I never thought she'd change his name and brainwash my child into being a criminal like her.

Now you need to make amends with the child you lost in the system, Malcolm stated. Then Kahlani called Harmony asking her to bring Dametrius and Jazz to the house? Within an hour Harmony, Jazz, Dametrius and Travion were in the living room staring at Jessica Stuart. Zeek looked at Dametrius in the eyes, placing a hand on his shoulder saying: this is Jessicca Stuart and she has information for you about the identity of your biological parents. We're here to support you in the situation son, Zeek said before giving Jessica the floor to speak.

Jessica stepped up to Dametrius nervously saying: I'm your biological mother, the woman that raised you was my friend. I didn't think she would use you for her crimes while I was in jail. What were you in jail for was all Dametrius had the strength to ask her. Turning toward Kahlani, Jessica replied, I was in jail for a long list of crimes against Mrs. Williams here. We were in high school when I helped Danella and your father along with another friend hold Kahlani hostage. It was the night of our Junior prom we raped and tortured her then we left her for dead on the floor thinking we'd never get caught. Knowing I was pregnant with you and finding out that Kahlani was pregnant as a result of your father raping her(sighing). Danella and I started stalking her and we jumped her in front of her house causing her to lose the baby.

Looking back and forth between his mother and the mother of one of his best friends sent Dametrius into sensory overload. Looking down he saw Harmony and Jazzlene wrapping their arms around him in comfort. Then he looked up at Jessica and asked: was the man that raised me my actual father? "Yes' ' was all Jessica said and Dametrius fell to his knees in a heap of tears. Sitting down next to her son Jessica repeatedly said "I'm sorry" while rocking him in her arms. Everyone in the room except Kahlani was shocked by this revelation from Kahlani's past.

On date night in February on the 21st all the couples were out having a good time when Cora started having Braxton Hicks at the table.

Max took her to the hospital within 10 minutes since it was close to World Tavern where they were eating. In 30 minutes Dr. Thompson showed up to check Cora and tell her it was a false alarm. From now until your due date I suggest you go on bed rest that means " no working, no stress,a low sodium diet and moderate exercise".This will help with labor and a smooth delivery, Dr.Thompson said before leaving.

19

3 arrive and 1 leaves

Max made sure Cora followed the doctor's orders everyday after leaving the hospital. At 5pm on March 5, 2023 Cora was feeling back pain so she took a bath. Just as she was finishing her bath there was a pop from her water breaking followed by contractions. "Max" she screamed in pain for him to come help her. As he got to the end of the hall Cora was putting on her shoes and calling Dr. Thompson's office. In a panic Max asked "Is it time"? With a nod of her head Max grabbed the bag out of the closet and headed for the front door. In 30 minutes they were at the hospital and in a room.

The attending doctor checked Cora to find that she was already dilated 3 cm. When Dr. Thompson arrived an hour later and checked Cora she was now at 5 cm. Okay Cora we're gonna get you to the O.R for surgery, Dr. Thompson replied heading for the door. "Surgery" why do I need surgery? Is something wrong with my babies? No Cora nothing is wrong with the babies at the moment but since your water has broken your babies are suffocating so we need to get them out fast.

In the O.R. Max was so nervous for his babies and the health of his fiance'. Everyone and everything in the room was moving so fast it made him dizzy. Then the doctor announced " here come baby A it's a boy and the nurse brought the munchkin over to Max to see. Do we have a name for this handsome fella the nurse asked? Yes, his name is

Alexander Maxwell Ramirez, Max Said with pride. And 5 minutes later baby B, Kaitlyn Vanessa Ramirez. Three minutes later baby C, Theresa Elise Ramirez came out screaming. Mom and dad got the chance to see them before they went to the nursery.

So on March 5, 2023 we got 3 new editions to the family at 11pm. Max called Zeek and Rashad to give them the news while Cora was resting after being stitched up. By 7am the whole gang was in the nursery to see the babies and falling in love with them. Before leaving Zeek helped Max give the babies baths and encouragement that he could do this parenting thing. Just as he got to the door Zeek turned around telling Max: don't panic just call me if you don't understand something. I sure will call you, you're the OG of having kids, Max said with a chuckle.

Ten days later Cora and the babies were free to go home with Max. As a surprise to Cora, Max enlisted the help of Rashad and Zeek to put together the nursery of her dreams for the babies. Walking into the house Cora saw it was clean and knew Kahlani had been in her home at some point. Then she walked down the hall toward the Master bedroom when the door to the nursery opened and Regina pulled her in. In complete amazement Cora sat the car seats down and thanked her friend for fixing up the nursery. Don't thank me for anything you should be thanking your man for this sis. That's when Cora noticed Max taking Alex out of his car seat in the corner. On that note Regina excused herself and went home to her man to give the Ramirez family privacy.

By April 2, 2023 Harmony and Kahlani were making flight and hotel reservations to Florida. Then Harmony called Travion with a question out of curiosity. Hey baby what can I do for you, Travion asked her. With a smile Harmony asked: do you have any plans in the next 8 days? "No" what's happening in 8 days baby, Travion asked confused. Well my biological mom is being executed in 8 days in Florida and wanted to know if you'd go with me for support. Say less wifey I'll be there, let get off this phone so I can book our flight, Travion said. With a chuckle

Harmony said, hubby I'm already booking our flight right now . I Love You wifey. I LoveYou too hubby.

When she hung up Harmony was met by the skeptical facial expression of Kahlani. With a giggle Harmony told her "Ma we're not married it's just how we saved our phone numbers in our contacts". At that point Kahlani couldn't even be mad because Zeek had done that during their courtship as well. Seven days later Harmony and Travion arrived at her parents home to pick them up for their trip. Malcolm and Kapri helped Janette and Michael take care of the younger ones until their return. At the airport one of the men Danella paid to break into Harmony's apartment tried to talk to her. Travion noticed and stepped in front of her angrily looking at the man saying "Antione why are you trying to put your hands on my woman"?

Hearing this Zeek stepped up asking: what's the problem over here. This is one of the men Danella paid to break into the apartment to rape Harmony and Jazzlene, Travion stated still angry. So let me ask you young man what business do you have with my daughter, Zeek asked looking the young man directly in the eye. At this point Harmony stepped away from the conversation to stand next to Kahlani. Just as Antoine was about to explain himself the announcement of their flight boarding came over the speaker. Zeek replied before walking away: If you dare to stalk or harass my daughter, just know her(father, brother, boyfriend and future father in law) are all cops. And I'm sure you already know Trey is a football player as well so don't set yourself up to get hurt by all of us at one time.

Two hours later the foursome landed in Florida and took the shuttle to their hotel. After resting they met up for dinner and everyone was concerned about how Harmony was holding up. In 11 hours her biological mother was going to be taking her last breath. Looking at everyone at the table Harmony told them: I'm fine, my concern is for Aunt Ella and my baby brother. Once dinner was over and they went to their rooms Harmony picked up her phone to call Aunt Ella about the situation.

Ella: Hello Harmony your brother wants to see you.

Harmony: I'll probably come spend the summer with him since I'll be in a wedding for two of Kahlani's friends. But I called you about what's taking place tomorrow morning.

Ella: What's happening tomorrow morning baby?

Harmony: My mother(Destiny) is being executed by lethal injection at 6am.

Ella: in a choked sob " what did your mother do? I thought she was already serving a life sentence.

Harmony: She conspired with 4 other inmates to try to kill Kahlani.

Ella: I'm sad by that news of what jealousy, greed, envy and hatred have led her to become. But you get some rest baby you have a tough day ahead of you tomorrow. Me and your brother love you, Good night.

Harmony: I Love You guys as well, Good Night

Harmony hung up and rolled over crying herself to sleep for 4 hours. Then it was 4:30 am and time to get ready to go with the prison being 30 minutes from the hotel. By 5 am Travion knocked on the door next to his room which belonged to Harmony. When she opened the door he could tell she didn't sleep well the night before. The drive to the prison Harmony was void of any emotion whatsoever. Once they arrived and were escorted to the viewing room everyone turned to check on her.

Then Destiny was brought into the room by two female guards. Then the doctor asked Destiny if she had anything to say to the people viewing her execution? Destiny turned her head to look at the glass window and locked eyes with Zeek first. With a flirty smile she said: I still and will always love you Officer Williams. Then she locked eyes with Harmony saying: I never wanted a daughter, all I wanted was a son that would look like your dad. Next she looked at the young man holding Harmony's hand and had a look of disgust on his face. Destiny told him " you can have her cause I don't and will ever want her". Lastly, she locked eyes with an angry Kahlani saying: I'm going to come back and drag you to the grave with me for stealing my man.

At this point everyone was offended by her words including the doctor in the room. The doctor looked over at Zeek who gave him a nod to proceed with execution. The first injection was administered to which Destiny had no reaction. Then the second injection was administered which made Destiny shed a single tear. Then the final injection was administered to which all the life disappeared from Destiny's eyes on the table. In a stoic manner Harmony led her parents and boyfriend out of the building toward the car. Back at the hotel they had lunch together then went back to their rooms. But Travion didn't go to his room, he went to Harmony's room where he found her crying by the door.

Picking her up Travion carried Harmony to the bed and sat down. That young man listened to his woman cry asking questions he didn't have the answers to for her. When she finally stopped crying he told her: She may not have wanted you but your dad did and I certainly do Wifey. Hearing him call her "wifey" brought a smile through the tears. With one peck on her lips he told her to go clean herself up so they could meet her parents for dinner. For 15 minutes Travion patiently waited for his lady to get ready. Takingher by the hand they walked to the elevator to meet Zeek and Kahlani in the lobby for dinner.

After having dinner on the beach the two couples went back to the hotel to get some rest since they'll be heading home tomorrow. That night again Harmony cried herself to sleep but this time was in the arms of her life partner. When that man said he would always be there for her he meant every word. By the next morning after breakfast everyone packed up to head to the airport. Upon seeing the sad state of their child Zeek and Kahlani were at a loss for words. After their 2 hour flight back to TN everyone felt so bad for Harmony. Kahlani even suggested that Harmony have a few sessions with the family therapist and take Travion for support.

With 5 wks until the wedding Harmony agreed and called the office of Dr. Wilson. Every Wednesday at 5 pm Harmony and Travion went to the sessions and even had some couples counseling. By the last week of May everyone was at the Egyptian Isles Resort for the wedding. All the ladies went up to the Queen's Suite where Cora and Regina were hanging out with her two daughters. Meanwhile Alexander was with his daddy and the rest of the men in their suite at the other end of the hall. Upon entering the suite all the ladies could hear Cora giggling on the phone with the groom.

Cora: How is Alex? Do you need me to send anything over with one of the girls?

Max: He's fine baby and if I need anything I'll send Zeek out the room. He's done this parent thing 6 times so I know he'll have all the answers for me.

Cora: I know that's right I still call Lani for everything

Max: The fellas are here so I'll talk to you later, I Love You

Cora: The girls just came in, I Love You too

20

Wedding Day

After 3 days of hanging out together and last minute preparations it was time for a wedding. And of course it wouldn't be a fun time without Janette putting on a show for everyone. Janette and Michael arrived the day before the wedding and got into an argument with the check-in clerk. Janette didn't like the room they had because it didn't have a beach view. Michael took her by the arm and told her " you don't need to look outside, just focus on me" with a flirty smile. I can do that most definitely but when you go to sleep afterwards I want a view of the city not a view of someone else's room.

Understanding what she meant the clerk checked and found one room available next to Zeek and Kahlani. Now happy with her room Janette settled down only to be in an argument with the housekeeper. Now she thought the lady was being too friendly with her son and husband in the hall. Sticking her head out the door Kahlani found an angry Janette yelling at the poor girl. Meanwhile her father in law and shirtless husband were trying to calm Janette down. Then she said fellas go inside let talk to Janette and the men looked at one another and shrugged. Once along Lani asked Janette why she was yelling at the young lady?

Janette explained that she asked Mike to stop her and get more towels. When he didn't come right back she came out to see what was taking so long. That's when she saw " this smurf" batting her eyes at Mike and about to place her hand on Zeek's crouch. If that's what really happened Lani could understand and react the same way. As hilarious as Janette made it sound, the only way to confirm anything is to watch the security footage at the resort. Later on that day all the girls met up at the spa to relax and Lani couldn't wait to talk about Janette. While getting their facials Lani asked: when you checked in did any of the staff get flirty with the guys in front of you? Harmony and Jazzlene said that the clerk was smiling too much at Dametrius and Travion. So how did you deal with that, Regina asked. In unison the ladies said " We kissed them right there in her face". Laughing and high fiving each other they asked: how about you Gina anything strange happen for you and Shad?

No because I told Mr. Officer I'd be committing a citizen's arrest of anyone who tries to ruin "My Wedding Day". Well I didn't have that problem when we checked in, Cora stated. Soon as they saw those 3 babies everyone knew he would be preoccupied until the end of this wedding. With a chuckle Lani said we didn't have a problem either but Janette sure did. All the ladies shouted " Oh Lord" what happened this time? Lani told the ladies what happened in the hallway upstairs and there wasn't a dry eye in the whole spa. Upstairs in the Men's suite Zeek told the fellas what happened and everyone looked over at Mike. Shaking his head with a chuckle he said " I don't know what I'm going to do with that woman" But I do know I can't live without her.

We feel the same way about our ladies but yours is the most entertaining Chief, Travion said with a laugh and the others followed. Let's hope she behaves herself tomorrow at the wedding, Zeek replied. Yes please, Gina has already warned me that she'd be making a citizen's arrest of anyone that ruins the wedding, Rashad stated shaking his head. Later that evening everyone got together for dinner on the beach and Janette brought her comedy too. When dinner was being served Janette was watching the servers closely. When the server sat a plate in front of Michael, she placed her other hand on his shoulder which both he and

Janette looked down at. Before he could ask the lady to move her hand Janette grabbed the lady by the wrist twisting it until it snapped making everyone cringe in pain.

All the other servers quickly placed the plates down and moved away. Whatever plans they had in mind to use on these men went out the window after that sighting. Now that Janette has made it clear exactly what will happen if you mess with any of these couples, let's call it a night and see what she does tomorrow at the wedding.

At last we made it to the second double wedding in this group. All the couples had breakfast together before parting ways to relax before the 4 pm wedding. Right on time everyone was outside at the pavilion for the ceremony. The entire bridal party was the picture of Old Hollywood Glam. Since Zeek's two youngest children were in the wedding Camille sat with Janette and Michael to watch over the triplets. By 4:15 the minister began by saying: these two beautiful couples would like to recite the vows they wrote for this moment.

Cora: I Cora Evelyn Fields takes Maximus Adam Ramirez to be my King. The last 2 yrs have been some of the best days of my life since I was a child. You have taken me from a Princess to a Queen as well as a mother. I will forever be grateful and thankful to God for you everyday. Here before these witnesses I pledge my Love and Devotion to you for the rest of our lives. I Love You.

Max: Maximus Adam Ramirez takes Cora Evelyn Fields as my life partner in this life and the next. The attraction I had for you 2 yrs ago and still have today will never change. I stand before these witnesses to promise this vow to you. I will Love, Honor and Obey you as the Queen of my heart and family. I Love You Forever.

Regina: On this day Regina Caroline Maxwell join my life with Rashad Linelle Lewis before these witnesses. From the day we met I fell in Love with the fact that you are a selfless man putting your life on the line for others. I've never felt safer than I do when you're around me. I vow on the 28th of May 2023 to be your Wife, Lover and Friend in word and deed. I Love You my King.

Rashad: Today Rashad Linelle Lewis welcomes Regina Caroline Maxwell into marriage with me. A marriage built on Honesty, Truth and Friendship between two souls. Nothing and No one can change the way I feel about you. As a man I accept God as my head so that I can lead you on the right path. Today I join my heart with yours Regina and entrust our marriage to God before these witnesses. I Love You my Queen.

There wasn't a dry eye around that courtyard even the minister was in tears hearing these words of the heart. Once he was able to compose himself he asked for the rings. 18 month old Brandon walked up to the minister with his hands in his pockets where the rings were. He pulled his little fists out and placed both sets of rings in the hands of the minister before walking back to his father. "Did I do good daddy"? he asked, holding Zeek's hand. You did great " Big Guy" Zeek told him with a smile. The minister then blessed the rings and the marriage of these lovely couples. Once the rings were placed on their hands the minister looked to his (left) saying: I now pronounce you Mr & Mrs Maximus Ramirez. Then he looked to his(right) saying: I now pronounce you Mr & Mrs Rashad Lewis. You gentlemen may now kiss your beautiful brides which they did without hesitation. Everyone clapped and cheered as the bridal party and couples walked to the other end of the courtyard to take photos before the reception.

21

A reception and a proposal

The rest of the guests made their way back into the resort to the reception hall that was covered in Red and White balloons and streamers. After getting drinks and finding their seats the announcement of the bridal party came from the DJ. Everyone turned to take pictures as the couples entered the event space. Once they were seated the DJ asked the best man and maid of honor to give their speeches. Being a gentleman Zeek passed the mic to his wife first before giving her a quick peck on the lips.

Kahlani: Max and Rashad what you just witnessed was a lesson in Happy Marriage 101. Cora and Regina you're the best sisters a girl could ever ask for. Regina I thank you for being the first person to welcome me into the education field. Then you introduced me to Cora who should have been a cop instead of a teacher. Don't be embarrassed now Cora, you knew my husband's whole life story before I did. Did you do a full background check on Max before you went on your first date? But aside from your great investigative work (you) Cora introduced me to my daughter Harmony so I guess you're a great matchmaker. I Love both of you ladies as my friends and my sisters, and I thank both of you fellas for taking them off the market. So they could stop asking if Zeek had any attractive friends in the force.

Zeek: Fellas I'm proud to call you my brothers in the force. Shad you were the first partner I had straight out of the academy. Thanks for putting up with my mother and Malcolm calling every night to keep us awake on the night shift. Max I was glad when they transferred you to our precinct. I didn't think I'd see you again after we left the academy. Now ladies I'm going to give you a little story about the men you married today. Before I met Lani these two told me I looked lonely and needed to go on a date. I told them I'd go if we went on a triple date. Our Captain got us all dates on Tinder as a joke. I got us a party bus so we wouldn't have to drive. When we showed up to pick up our dates, these two fools took one look at the girls and I quote "we'd be better off dating a middle or high school teacher". At least they'd know better than to go outside wearing halloween costumes in the summertime. Rashad's date was dressed like a Nun while Max's date was dressed like the bride of Frankenstien and mine looked like the bride of Chucky. Needless to say that date was over in 2.5 seconds when Rashad put the girls out the bus and told the driver to just keep driving. I asked what we were going to tell the captain about this date. Max looked at me with a straight face saying: he can keep his lineup for himself, we are not going to entertain or investigate those unusual suspects ever again. By September I showed up late to pick Harmony up from school and behold I spotted Cora talking with Lani and my daughter. Now it was my turn to start plotting so I called Max and asked if he remembered what he and Rashad said about dating teachers? Now look at us all married to Middle School Teachers and becoming dads. Well, Rashad isn't there yet but I've given Max parenting advice so you can ask him for advice and only call me for a second opinion.

Now it was time for dinner to be served and thank God Janette had no complaints . Every member of the bridal party was ready for Janette to put on a show about Chef Jean not catering this wedding. But the food was made by the families of the Brides and Grooms so she held her peace. After dinner it was time for the first dance of Rashad and Regina

Lewis. The sound of Howard Hewett "Once, Twice, Three Times" came over the speakers. As the song came to an end the DJ asked them to stay on the floor as he called Max and Cora for their first dance. Now the soulful sound of Major's "Why I Love You" came over the speakers. Next the rest of the bridal party was called to the dance floor as the smooth sound of Alicia Keys "Un-thinkable" began to play. As the song came to an end everyone noticed that Travion was down on one knee in front of Harmony with a 4-carat heart shaped diamond ring in hand. There was no need for him to say anything because with tears in her eyes Harmony shouted her answer of Yes. After the cutting of the cake and dessert was served everyone congratulated Harmony and Travion before heading home.

On the way back to their room at the resort Kahlani told Zeek how much she loved his speech. The two laughed at stories about their friends until they got into bed. Before going to sleep Kahlani asked Zeek: isn't it crazy that our two oldest children have moved out and are about to get married? Yeah baby it really is crazy but I'm proud of them finding their equal partners in life. I'm sure they're going to ask us to help with the weddings and as their father I'll be glad to. Turning over to face her husband Kahlani saying: as their mother I'll be glad too as well and their siblings can also be involved. Then they drifted off to dreamland until 6 hrs later when it was time to pack up their children and head home.

On the drive home Brandon asked his mom and Christian if he did a good job in the wedding? You sure did little bro, Christian said while giving him a fist bump. Looking over her shoulder with a smile saying: mommy is so proud of you baby boy you looked so handsome up there. Brandon's face lit up with him saying: just like daddy. Kahlani glanced over at Zeek who was driving saying: just as handsome as daddy and brother. Just as the family pulled into the driveway the police captain was parked in front of their home.

Captain, what are you doing here? Is something wrong that I need to know, Zeek asked concerned? Nothing serious. I was just checking to see if your son was still going to his mother's execution. And to let you know that Calvin Donaldson's sentence has been reduced to Life in Prison. Lastly, to give you this letter from New York's Women's Prison about Alexis it came to the station for you.

22

Another execution and 2 honeymoons

Thanks for bringing the letter to me Captain and Yes Malcolm is going to Melody's execution. My wife and I are going for moral support as well as his fiance'. Let me get my crew into the house and I'll see you at the station tomorrow. After getting settled in the house Zeek told Kahlani about his conversation with the Captain outside. Kahlani called Jessica to let her know that her baby daddy got a reduced sentence. Sitting on the couch they both read the letter about Alexis Mitchell being killed in an altercation with her cell mate.

Meanwhile over in Paris Regina and Rashad were relaxing in their honeymoon suite. Then there was a knock at the door and the two of them went to the door together to answer it. On the other side was the girl Zeek talked about in his speech. Rashad looked shocked to see her delivering room service and still looking like the bride of Frankenstien. Regina couldn't understand his look of shock so she asked if he knew the woman?

Baby that's the date Zeek was talking about in his speech at the wedding, Rashad said. Really, I see she hasn't changed her costume in years, Regina said before they both began to laugh. After having their dinner it was time for dessert and by dessert I mean Regina. It was time to consummate their marriage all over that suite. For the next 2 days they stayed at the resort to partake in onsite activities but Rashad's past was everywhere they went on the resort. For the next three days their concierge had a tour guide take Mr & Mrs Lewis around the city.

Shopping in the city of Paris was like going to fashion week in every store. When they returned to the resort everyday that woman seemed to be stalking them or mostly just Rashad. Regina caught her trying to pick pocket Rashad while they were waiting for the elevator to go up to their room. Then when they got to their room someone had gone through their luggage and torn up all of Regina's clothes except her wedding dress and lingerie. And there were lipstick stains on Rashad's shirts and underwear.

On the 6th day of their honeymoon it was time to talk with management and security. After watching the camera footage it was clear who was in their room. Needless to say she was terminated from her job and arrested for stalking Rashad and harrassing Regina. The final 4 days of their honeymoon was peaceful and fun wrapped in each other's embrace. As they were packing to go home Regina was very nauseous and couldn't even finish packing without Rashad's help.

Over in Italy Max and Cora sat in a gondola for an evening ride around Florence after they landed. The second day the two went on a tour of Venice. By the 3rd day they had come from touring Naples when a strange woman with goth makeup approached them. After taking a closer look at the woman Max screamed and ran for the elevator telling Cora to get away from that woman NOW. Finally in their room Cora asked: what was that all about? Do you know her or something?

Baby do you remember that story Zeek told at the wedding about the bride of Chucky? Yes I remember but what does that have to do with her? Cora that was her downstairs in the lobby, the question is how did she know we would be staying here? On the next day Mr & Mrs Ramirez went on a tour of Rome, they ordered room service and noticed the same lady at the end of the hall. Once they finished eating Cora became increasingly sick. By the morning a doctor was called to check on Cora only to find out that she was poisoned. Only one suspect had Max's antennas up and he explained to management and the Italian Police what he believed happened .

After speaking with the room service attendant it was clear who had poisoned Cora and wanted her out of the way. For the next two days Cora was in bed resting while Max helped the Police track down their suspect in her poisoning. By the 6th day their suspect was seen lurking around the resort looking for Max . She even claimed that she was his 2nd wife and needed to get into his room to talk to him.

For the remaining 4 days their honeymoon was filled with romance. Their culprit was taken into custody for attempted murder and stalking. Then it was time to go back home to Tennessee and back to their triplets. 14 days was too long for them to be away from their newborns. As for the Lewis family, 14 days may have been enough time for their culprit to escape and bother them some more.

While this was going on Malcolm and Kapri, joined by Zeek and Kahlani made their way to Colorado for Melody's execution. After landing at Denver International Airport and using a shuttle to their hotel the two couples sat down for lunch. Again Zeek and Kahlani were having a pep talk with one of their children about watching a part of their existence dying by lethal injection. Malcolm tried to convince them that he was fine; they had nothing to worry about. They, along with Kapri knew he was lying but went along with it.

The following day at 7 am on the 14th of June it was time to say goodbye to the parent he never got to know. That was the part that bothered Malcolm the most about this day. Once they arrived at the prison and were brought to the viewing room the sight of the table way gave Malcolm the finality of the situation. Standing between his father and fiance' Malcolm watched his mother be brought into the room.

Once she was strapped to the table Melody was asked if she had anything to say to her visitors.

Looking up to the window made eye contact with Kapri and smiled. Thank you for making my son happy and congrats on your engagement. Then she looked at her son to say: I'm sorry for leaving you behind, I wasn't ready to be a mom back then. Next she made eye contact with Zeek and smiled saying: I did and still do love you. You're a great father and did a great job raising our son. Lastly; Melody locked eyes with Kahlani and began to scowl saying; I guess I should thank you for taking care of the two men I love. Don't get it twisted I still hate you and wish I can come back from the dead to kill you.

The guard said that was enough talking from her at this point and told her to lay down on the table. Now it was time for the doctor to do his job of ending her life. The injection went in smoothly with Melody not even flinching. Then the second injection went in and Malcolm watched closely as a tear rolled down toward her left ear. the little boy in Malcolm wanted to go wipe that tear away and tell her it was going to be okay. When the final injection went in and Melody's body jerked before laying still on the table is when Malcolm fell apart in his father's arms.

The man understood what had just happened but that little boy in Malcolm still wanted to know what changed and made her become a bad person. Why did she hate Kahlani so much? Why didn't she come back to be a family sooner so all his siblings could have the same mom? At this point we just like Malcolm will never get the answer to those questions. After letting Malcolm pour out all his pain of seeing his mother die it was time to head back to the hotel.

The whole ride back Malcolm was stoic with a solemn expression on his face. We got to the hotel Malcolm walked straight to the elevator holding Kapri's hand with his parents not far behind. Once on their floor Zeek and Kahlani hugged them saying: we'll see you in the morning for check out. In the room Malcolm just laid in the bed silently filled with sorrow. By the next morning Malcolm was numb from his sorrow. Yet when they got home he'd have better things to concern himself with, mainly his wedding to Kapri.

The whole flight home Zeek and Kahlani watched with concern as Malcolm laid in Kapri's arms not saying anything to anyone. As they pulled up to the house Malcolm just looked like he was going to fall apart at any moment. Camille and Ann Marie went over to his house next door to visit. Mally you look sad, who made you cry, the girls asked? Big brother is okay but someone wanted to hurt mommy and they died yesterday, Malcolm said holding his sisters hands. So mommy is safe now right brother, Ann Marie asked curiously? She sure is munchkin and so are you, Malcolm stated with a smile. Both the girls shouted "Yay" as they went back over to their home next door. That made Malcolm feel better just seeing his sisters smile and happy.

23

The Final chapter

A week later both the Ramirez and Lewis families came over to Zeek's home to hang out. How was the honeymoon for both of you, Michael asked. Funny you mention that because something unfortunate happened to both of us on our honeymoon, Max replied. What happened? Was it anything like ours, Janette asked, being nosey. Everyone took a seat to hear this story cause they knew it would be a good one. Y'all remember that story Zeek told at the wedding about our tinder dates, Rashad asked? Everyone replied "Yeah Why". Rashad took a breath and responded because our dates from that night showed up on our honeymoons.

I know you are lying Bro, Kahlani said, shocked at the news. No we're not sis, Rashad replied looking uncomfortable talking about the whole situation. Then he told his story of how the girl tried to make them dinner and he gave it to the couple in the room next door. So what did you have for dinner, Harmony asked? I ordered doordash for us to eat. It was still good food. Regina even caught the girl trying to pickpocket me and grab my butt while we were waiting for the elevator.

See I told you I wasn't being extra about how these lonely heifers be acting around a man that's taken, Janette said getting riled up. She even broke into our room and cut up all of Gina's clothes except the wedding dress and lingerie. She took pictures of herself in them then she put lipstick stains on all of my clothes. Needless to say we had to buy new clothes just to wear home. That's messed up unc, Malcolm said but does she still look like the bride of Frankenstien? She's the Gothic version but still ugly nonetheless, Rashad exclaimed.

Well that sucked but did she follow you everywhere in the city, Max asked? Nah, just around the resort our tour guide knew all the shortcuts to keep us undetected off the resort. You're lucky cause that chucky looking girl followed us to every city in Italy. She even put rat poison in our room service order. Then she told the front desk that she was my first wife and they gave her a key to our room. Then she put rat poison in all the drinks in the mini bar and nearly killed Cora after drinking one bottle of water with her dinner. I had to wait an hour for a doctor to come take care of Cora while I worked with the cops to take her into custody. The whole time she kept saying Cora was the imposter when it was really her.

That's crazy man now I'm sorry for sharing that story at your wedding, Zeek said sadly. Don't blame yourself Zeek you didn't this would happen, Rashad replied. Do you think the captain did this to us for putting them out of the bus all those years ago, Max asked? Maybe I'm not sure but he was acting strange in my opinion, Zeek stated. What do you mean by strange son, Mike asked concerned. Well after the wedding he was sitting outside in front of the house when I pulled up with the family. He didn't even call to say he needed to speak to me about anything, Zeek said worriedly. I asked why he was here and he said my mail was sent to the station and came to drop it off.

Why would my mail be sent to the station and not be in my mailbox here so I checked the mailbox and all the mail from the previous week was still there. After I sent Lani and the kids in the house I asked him why he was really here. He told me that he came to personally let me know that Calvin's sentence has been reduced to Life in Prison and that Alexis Mitchell was killed by her cellmate in a fight. Couldn't he have told you that over the phone, Cora asked? I think we need to put eyes on your captain because this isn't ethical at all and could be dangerous, Mike proclaimed. He might even start harassing Malcolm at the station just to get under your skin.

I think we have a lot of questions for Captain when we get to work and I know he's going to lie to us, Rashad said shaking his head. But on a high note we just found out Regina is pregnant, Rashad exclaimed. All the ladies in the house started jumping around and cheering for them. Congrats my boy, Zeek said with a smile. Now you can ask Zeek for advice on being a dad, Max said with a smirk.

Now we have come to the end of one series and we're going to start another. With two weddings coming up in the Williams Family we'll dive into the Bonded by Love Series for 2025. we'll see if the Captain will try to start trouble with Malcolm and Zeek. We'll also see if Christian finds a girlfriend now that he's in high school.

It was a pleasure writing this series for all of my fiction readers out there. I hope you will continue to go on these relatable fiction roller coaster rides with me.

K.Moore

Don't miss out!

Visit the website below and you can sign up to receive emails whenever K.Moore publishes a new book. There's no charge and no obligation.

https://books2read.com/r/B-A-DOREB-FSLMD

BOOKS 2 READ

Connecting independent readers to independent writers.